A Song of Stars

A SONG

Holiday House / New York

OF STARS

An Asian legend adapted by

TOM BIRDSEYE

illustrated by

JU-HONG CHEN

For my father, Irving Birdseye,
who believed in love and a world of soft songs.
TOM BIRDSEYE

To my wife, Lin Zheng-Fei
JU-HONG CHEN

In the shining night sky, beside the great expanse of the river of stars called the Milky Way, lived a beautiful young princess named Chauchau. Daughter of the Emperor of the Heavens, she lived in a small house perched on the edge of her very own star.

Chauchau was a weaver—not of wool or silk, but of the shimmering threads of the firmament. Working at her loom, she intertwined fibers of moonglow and starlight into gleaming robes for the sky dwellers. She was happy and always young, singing soft songs only the cloth could hear as she worked.

But that was before the herdsman, Newlang, wandered by, gently prodding an ox with his staff, singing soft songs only an ox could hear. Chauchau looked up from her weaving and saw a clear brightness in the young man.

Newlang looked up and saw the same in the princess. Both left their work and walked together beside the great expanse of the Milky Way. Soon they sang the same soft song, a song of love for all to hear.

For the Emperor of the Heavens, the love his daughter and the herdsman shared was a fine thing to see—strong and sure, full of trust and warmth. He called Chauchau and Newlang to his throne and announced that they should be married.

But soon the lovers became devoted only to each other and always being together. Work gave way to long walks hand in hand beside the river of stars. Duty was replaced by soft kisses while sitting in the lap of the moon. The ox wandered about untended, nibbling light from any star it pleased. The loom lay still and silent, no longer weaving threads of the firmament into gleaming robes for the sky dwellers.

Then the Emperor of the Heavens became angry, and again called Chauchau and Newlang before him. "You have forsaken duty by caring only for one another," he said. "Though it pains me greatly to do so, it is my burden to punish such behavior. You must be separated—my daughter, Chauchau, to live on one side of the Milky Way, Newlang, the herdsman, on the other. Only once a year, on the seventh night of the seventh month, will you be allowed to cross the river of stars and meet." The Emperor of the Heavens looked out with sad eyes. "So it is decreed."

From that day on, the Milky Way became a barrier between the two lovers. Chauchau sat on one bank, again weaving at her loom, while across the flickering stream of light, Newlang prodded the ox gently with his staff. Both sang soft songs as they worked, songs that only an ox and loom could hear. Both waited for the seventh night of the seventh month.

Many times during the year, the princess weaver would go down to the bank of the river of stars and look across for a glimpse of the man she loved. But often the same clouds that could so easily fly over the starry current would block her view and she would cry out in loneliness.

So it was for Newlang also. He saw Chauchau rarely—a fleeting hint of her long sleeve waving in the same breeze that touched his cheek, the glint of her night thread on the loom as it reflected the light of the same moon that lit his sorrow . . .

until, at last, the seventh night of the seventh month arrived. Newlang rushed to a small boat he had hidden behind the moon and pulled it to the bank of the Milky Way. Across the blinking starway he could see Chauchau. She had waded into the river up to her knees, the wet trail of her robe swirling around her like a watery rainbow, her face glowing with beauty and joy.

Newlang pushed the small boat away from the bank and paddled
with strong, sure strokes for the other side. Surging over the waves,
his paddle sent mists of spray into the air.

But soon it began to rain—first only a few small drops, leaving tiny circles here and there on the surface of the river. Then, as Newlang paddled, the raindrops grew larger and closer together, and the tiny circles became larger, also rippling out from their centers until the water seemed to boil under the curtain of a pounding storm.

The river began to swell; the rain continuing even harder. Quickly, the gentle flow of the Milky Way became a raging torrent, sending waves rolling over one another and crashing into an angry tide of stars.

Chauchau was knocked from her feet and barely pulled herself to the safety of the shore. She turned and watched in despair as Newlang's small boat rose to the crest of a giant wave and flipped over into the heart of the storm. Through the curtain of rain and waves she saw him struggle back to his side of the river. Then her tears washed all sight of him away. The seventh night of the seventh month was almost over. They would have to wait for another whole year.

Although the Emperor of the Heavens had separated his daughter and the herdsman, their love was still a fine thing for him to see—strong and sure, full of trust and warmth. It was then that he sent forth the Magpie King and his flock to the banks of the swollen Milky Way.

The magpies swooped above the weeping princess. Then, in a swirling spiral of wings, they stretched up, up into the farthest reaches of the stars, across the Milky Way, and touched down on the other bank.

Chauchau looked out over the river to see a gently rustling bridge of birds, their wings spread tip to tip in an arch across the river.

Within minutes the princess weaver was in Newlang's arms. Even if only for a short time, they were together, singing the same soft song of love for all to hear.

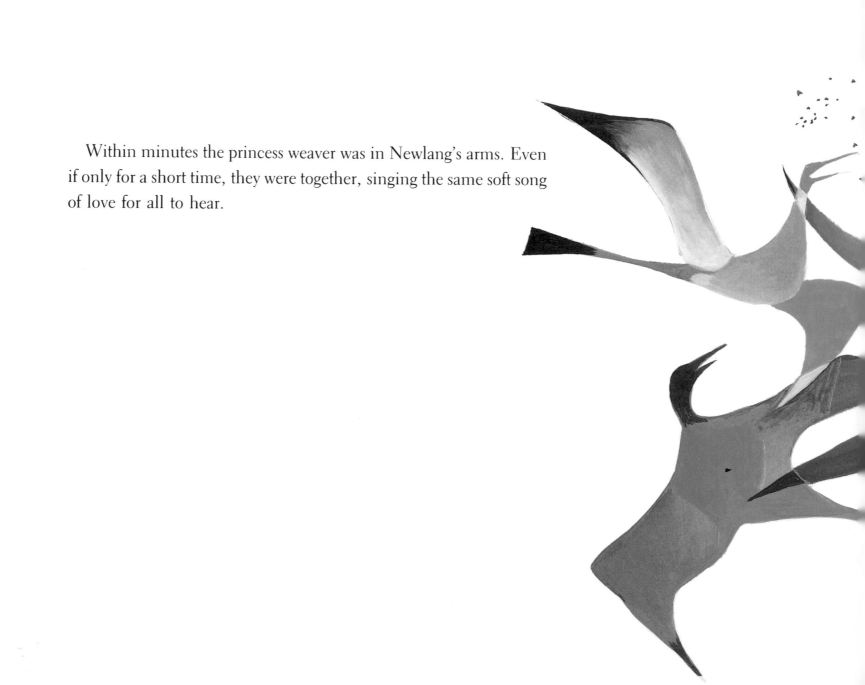

AUTHOR'S NOTE

On the seventh night of the seventh month, the people of China celebrate the ancient story of the stars Vega (the princess weaver) and Altair (the herdsman), separated on either side of the Milky Way. It is called Chi Hsi, the Festival of the Milky Way.

The myth and celebration have also spread to other parts of Asia. In Japan, the princess weaver is called Shokujo, the herdsman Kengyu, and the festival the Tanabata, or Weaving Loom Festival.

In both countries, the celebration is in honor of the annual reunion of the herdsman and the princess weaver. In both it is in honor of love.

Incense is offered in China. In Japan, large bamboo poles are cut and set up in front of houses and stores, then hung with elaborate decorations, and love poems that are written on colored paper. Chinese women and girls pray for skill in handiwork. School children in Japan present samples of their best calligraphy. Fruit, melons, sweets, and cakes are offered to the stars in both countries, as are hopes for fair skies. For if it is rainy on the seventh night of the seventh month, the drops are called "a rain of tears." The river of stars is flooded and the herdsman cannot get across. The princess weaver weeps in sadness. The magpies have yet to come and make a bridge of wings across the Milky Way. But if it is calm and clear, many say they can see mists of spray in the sparkling night sky. It is from the herdsman's oar as he paddles his small boat across the great expanse of the Milky Way. Strong and sure, he glides over the waves, into the waiting arms of the princess weaver, where together they sing the same soft song of love for all to hear.

Library of Congress Cataloging-in-Publication Data

Birdseye, Tom.
　　A song of stars / written by Tom Birdseye; illustrated by
　Ju-Hong Chen. — 1st ed.
　　　　p.　　cm.
　　Summary: Although banished to opposite sides of the Milky Way, the princess weaver and the herdsman reunite each year on the seventh day of the seventh month.
　　ISBN 0-8234-0790-X
　　[1. Folklore—China.　2. Milky Way—Folklore.　3. Stars—Folklore.]　I. Chen, Ju-Hong, ill.　II. Title.
PZ8.1.B534So　1990　　　89-20066　　　CIP　　　AC
398.26—dc20
[E]